THE DRAGON
WHO ATE OUR SCHOOL

Nick Toczek works as a poet, storyteller,
journalist, lecturer, political researcher, novelist and
stand-up comedian. He has made almost 20,000
public appearances over the past 30 years and most
recently has toured his *Dragons!* show which includes
a real Chinese parading dragon and a smoke machine.

For more information on Nick Toczek,
check out his website at
http://www.poems.fsnet.co.uk

THE DRAGON WHO ATE OUR SCHOOL

Poems

by Nick Toczek

Illustrated by Sally Townsend

MACMILLAN
CHILDREN'S BOOKS

First published 1995 as *Dragons* by Macmillan Children's Books

This edition published 2002 for the
Book People Ltd,
Hall Wood Avenue,
Haydock, St Helens WA11 9UL

Associated companies throughout the world

ISBN 0 330 34829 9

Text copyright © Nick Toczek 1995
Illustrations copyright © Sally Townsend 1995

The right of Nick Toczek to be identified as the
author of this work has been asserted by him in accordance
with the Copyright, Designs and Patents Act 1988.

7 9 8

A CIP catalogue record for this book is available from
the British Library.

Printed and bound in Great Britain by
Mackays of Chatham plc, Chatham, Kent

Contents

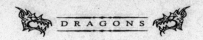

The Dragon's Curse

Enter darkness. Leave the light.
Here be nightmare. Here be fright.
Here be dragon, flame and flight.
Here be spit-fire. Here be grief.
So curse the bones of unbelief.
Curse the creeping treasure-thief.
Curse much worse the dragon-slayer.
Curse his purse and curse his payer.
Curse these words. Preserve their sayer.
Earth and water, fire and air.
Prepare to meet a creature rare.
Enter, now, if you dare.
Enter, now . . . the dragon's lair!

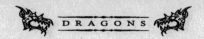

The Child Who Pretended to be a Dragon

My mum and dad got angry
and they told me not to lie,
when I said that I'd grown wings
and was learning how to fly.

They said I should be sensible
and stop making a fuss,
after I'd announced that I was green
and longer than a bus.

And they turned around and told me
I was not to tell tall tales,
when they heard that I'd been claiming
that my skin was growing scales.

Then both of them got cross with me
and each called me a liar,
just because I mentioned
I'd been breathing smoke and fire.

But they finally got flaming mad,
they really hit the roof,
when I rushed at them with sharpened claws
and all my teeth, as proof.

My mum let out a piercing scream.
My dad began to rave.
So I ate them both. They tasted nice.
Then I flew off to live in a cave.

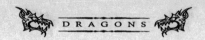

Dragon

Dragon has spikes all down her back,
has claws in her paws that she draws to attack.
She's scaly, savage and sickly green,
merciless, mindless, cruel and mean.

Dragon is heartless, has no soul.
Her red eyes glow like burning coal.
A body that's built with bullet-proof scales.
She can pound you to pulp with a swish of her tail.

Dragon has a furnace fitted in each lung,
a flickering, forked and fireproof tongue,
crocodile jaws from which she pours
great searing flames, with frightful roars.

Dragon's cave is a reeking trench
with a dank, sulphurous, smoky stench
made fouler by the crevices and cracks
where rotting limbs are stored for snacks.

Dragon loves her cavernous lair,
keeps her heaps of treasures there,
hardly sleeps for fear of thieves,
needs to be ravenous before she leaves.

When dragon spreads her dreadful wings
death will be what her hunger brings.
Breathlessly, she pursues warm flesh.
She wants it human, young and fresh.

Dragon spies people far beneath.
She flies down, claws first, followed by teeth.
She grips and grinds. She chomps and chews.
She spits out belt-buckles, buttons and shoes.

Dragon finally finishes feeding
splattered red from all their bleeding,
flies home slowly with a bloated gut,
reaches the entrance to her darkness . . . but . . .

Dragon senses men and horses,
sniffs the air . . . sniffs then pauses . . .
A stink, she thinks, not normally there . . .
A man, somewhere inside her lair!

When a dragon stares into her breath,
her life up to the point of death
appears before her in the smoke –
the future pulling back its cloak.

Dragon breathes . . . The picture clears
but lacks its usual months and years.
Instead she sees reflected back
mere moments, then a sea of black.

Dragon slayer draws his bow,
aims, and lets his arrow go.
It flies to where the scaly coat
is weakest, at the creature's throat.

Dragon feels the fatal flood,
the sea of black, the flow of blood,
and far below, the undertow
of pain, from bolt and piercing blow.

Dragon falls and twists about.
Her fire chokes and flickers out.
She coughs a cloud of smoke. She sighs,
then lies quite still, with staring eyes.

The slayer slices off her head
to make quite certain that she's dead.
These killings bring him little pleasure.
He never dares to touch their treasure.

He doesn't like the job as such.
It doesn't earn him very much.
And with each dragon, goes a curse.
So death by death, his life grows worse.

Why does he do it, you may ask?
Well, someone has to do the task.
He breaks her eggs. He blocks her cave.
He buries her body in a shallow grave,
shoves the head in a blood-stained sack
and leads his horse back down the track.

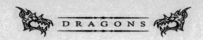

Roaring Like Dragons

On the count of four, I want you all to roar.
One . . . two . . . three . . . four . . .

No! Not the squawk of a fowl,
or the hoot of an owl,
or the half-choked note of a bleating goat,
or the moody moo that a cow'll do.
That was very, very poor.
I fare better when I snore.
What I want is a *proper* roar.
One . . . two . . . three . . . four . . .

No, no, no! Not a toothsome scowl,
or a long, loud vowel,
or the screech of creatures
when a beast is on the prowl.
Call that your best? I'm far from sure.
It didn't thrill me to the core.
Now gimme a roar I can't ignore.
One . . . two . . . three . . . four . . .

Pathetic! Did I ask for a yell or a yelp or a yowl?
Did I call for a caterwaul, holler or howl,
or a burp or a belch
from a belly or a bowel?
Now rattle the windows and the door.
Shake the ceiling and the floor.

Show your jaw what your lungs are for.
One . . . two . . . three . . . four . . .

Hmm. That felt fierce and forcefully foul.
I'd call that a fabulously fearsome growl.
But did it rip your lips up?
No! Did it jellify your jowl?
No! Well, sorry to be a bit of a bore.
But I think you can guess what I've got in store . . .
that I'm going to ask you for even more.
So be louder than the crowd when the home team
    score.
Make a shock-wave worse than the Third World
    War.
Do astounding sounds, like dragons galore.
Roar and roar as never before.
Roar and roar till your throats are sore.
One . . . two . . . three . . . four . . .

Encore!

Encore!!

Encore!!!

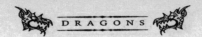
The Dragon Who Ate Our School

– 1 –

The day the dragon came to call,
she ate the gate, the playground wall
and, slate by slate, the roof and all,
the staffroom, gym, and entrance hall,
and every classroom, big or small.

So . . .
She's undeniably great.
She's absolutely cool,
the dragon who ate
the dragon who ate
the dragon who ate our school.

– 2 –

Pupils panicked. Teachers ran.
She flew at them with wide wingspan.
She slew a few and then began
to chew through the lollipop man,
two parked cars and a transit van.

Wow . . . !
She's undeniably great.
She's absolutely cool,
the dragon who ate
the dragon who ate
the dragon who ate our school.

– 3 –

She bit off the head of the head.
She said she was sad he was dead.
He bled and he bled and he bled.
And as she fed, her chin went red
and then she swallowed the cycle shed.

Oh . . .
She's undeniably great.
She's absolutely cool,
the dragon who ate
the dragon who ate
the dragon who ate our school.

– 4 –

It's thanks to her that we've been freed.
We needn't write. We needn't read.
Me and my mates are all agreed,
we're very pleased with her indeed.
So clear the way, let her proceed.

Cos . . .
She's undeniably great.
She's absolutely cool,
the dragon who ate
the dragon who ate
the dragon who ate our school.

A Rave in a Cave

I was snugglin' down in a smugglers' cavern
when in came a hagglin' gaggle of dragons.
They were gigglin' an' braggin'
an' smug about a muggin'
in which they did a thug in
gave the mug a sluggin'
an' legged it with the loot the lout was luggin'.

The gaggle of dragons
were draggin' in a wagon.
The wagon had a bag on
and the bag had their swag in.
Swag is what dragons crave.
An' as they gathered there together in the cave
their pleasure with their treasure
was more than I could measure.
An' they love a life of leisure
so they launched into a rave in the cave.

A zig-zaggin' ragamuffin
druggy drunken dragon
was staggerin' around
an' swiggin' from a flagon.
They were all so unsavoury
braggin' of their bravery
an' gravely misbehavin'
the way they took to ravin'
the day they took to ravin'
the day they gave a rave
in their favourite cave.

An' a swaggerin' stag
of a dressed-up dragon
was gettin' quite an agonisin' slaggin'
from the chin-waggin' naggin'
great gob with a fag in
of a raggedy haggard
an' scraggy old bag of a dragon.
But they both soon forgot an' forgave
cos the cave rave
the dragons gave
was a helluva hearty party.

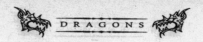
An' a raggle-taggle dragon,
all bedraggled an' gaggin',
was blaggin' odd drags
of the old bag's fags
an' swiggin' from the ragamuffin's flagon.
An' everybody got so depraved
on the day that the dragons
day that the dragons
day that the dragons raved.

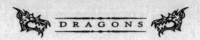
The American Dragon

Elephantine, with a burger belly,
he sits in New York, watching telly –
a graceless beast in a room that's smelly.

This figure far bigger than a Botticelli
is fed fatty food from his local deli,
fries and pizzas and tagliatelli.

His weak wings flap like a pair of umbrelli
for a flightless wobble by a bright green jelly
with more spare tyres than anyone requires . . .
. . . even the suppliers of Pirelli!

He's jealous of the elegance of Gene Kelly
and longs to be lithe like Lisa Minnelli
or to flaunt a physique like football's Pele.

But elephantine, with a burger belly,
he sits in New York, watching telly –
this graceless beast in a room that's smelly.

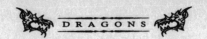

What Have We Got in the House?

I think I know what we've got in the house.
When it moves, it makes more mess than a mouse.
So, what do you think we've got in the house?

We found egg-shell down
By the washing machine
And four claw-prints
In the margarine.

I think I know what we've got in the house.
When it moves, it makes more mess than a mouse,
Or a rat, or a roach, or a louse.
So, what do you think we've got in the house?

The sides of the bath
Are greenish-tinged
And the spare toothbrush
Has had its bristles singed.

I think I know what we've got in the house.
When it moves, it makes more mess than a mouse.
Or a rat, or a roach, or a louse,
Or a gerbil, or an oyster, or a grouse.
So, what do you think we've got in the house?

We've never had a fire
But I often cough.
Then the smoke alarm
In the hall goes off.

I think I know what we've got in the house.
When it moves, it makes more mess than a mouse.
Or a rat, or a roach, or a louse,
Or a gerbil, or an oyster, or a grouse,
Or a duck-billed platypus together with its spouse.
So, what do you think we've got in the house?

There are long scratch-marks
Just like from claws
Around the handles
Of all the doors.

I think I know what we've got in the house.
Don't you?

Modern Dragons

Modern dragons act all flash,
swish around with wads of cash,
splash out rashly, dish the dosh,
push for posh and pricey nosh.

They've more money than they've senses,
have expensive residences,
high-class caves to suit the choosy –
bidet, sauna and jacuzzi.
Wall-to-wall, these works of art
are sumptuous, deluxe and smart.

Modern dragons of both sexes
need fine jewellery, nice Rolexes,
diamonds on their necks and wrists,
gold rings clustered round their fists,
pearl-encrusted treasure chests
thrust in niches in their nests.

Modern dragons, draped in jewels,
laze by heated swimming pools,
sip Bacardis and Martinis,
lounge around in Lamborghinis.
There's not much they can't afford
and all their claws are manicured.

Modern dragons own race horses,
drive to parties in green Porsches
or Ferraris or Rolls Royces,
talk in crisp and cultured voices,
carve out consonant and vowel.
Modern dragons never growl.

With body-lines all re-defined
our dragons now are quite refined.
They've had their awkward wings removed.
They call it 'surgically improved'.
They've also been unspiked, untailed,
their skins made paler and de-scaled,
body-fat redistributed,
teeth filed flat, false hair recruited.

Snake-skin booted, silken suited,
they socialise, their fire muted.

Modern dragons cruise and jet.
They never work. They never sweat.
Their world is one devoid of debt
where anything they want, they get –
a world so small, there is no threat.
They never need to get upset.
The only things that make them fret
are status, style and etiquette.

Raggin' the Dragon

We come right up to the mouth of the cave.
We shout for him as if we're brave.
And he hates the way that we behave.
We make him rant. We make him rave.

We're raggin' the dragon.
We're raggin' the dragon.
We're givin' the dragon some agony.

Raggin' the dragon is second-to-none.
It's all a game we learn for fun.
We call a name. We turn and run.
We shout: –

'Old slug!
Scabby Lug!
Cave bug!
Ugly thug!

Bag on your head.
Bag on your head.
Face like a dragon,' we said.

Raggin' the dragon is second-to-none.
It's all a game we learn for fun.
We call a name. We turn and run.

We shout: –
'Worm tail!
Beached whale!
Hook nail!
Smelly snail!'

Slaggin' you off.
Slaggin' you off.
'Call yourself a dragon?' we scoff.

Raggin' the dragon is second-to-none.
It's all a game we learn for fun.
We call a name. We turn and run.
We shout: –

'Stink pot!
Body rot!
Hot snot!
Grumpy grot!'

Smack in the snout.
Smack in the snout.
'Raggedy dragon,' is what we shout.

Raggin' the dragon is second-to-none.
It's all a game we learn for fun.
We call a name. We turn and run.
We shout: –

'Green yob!
Slimy slob!
Big blob!
Toothy gob!

Gag on your tongue.
Gag on your tongue.
Voice like a dragon,' we sung.

Raggin' the dragon is second-to-none.
It's all a game we learn for fun.
We call a name. We turn and run.

We're raggin' the dragon.
We're raggin' the dragon.
We're givin' the dragon some agony.

Dancing Dragons

The British dragons' trip to France
is just a chance to drink and dance.
They booze in the bars on the ferry,
get very merry on duty-free sherry
and bottles of champagne perry.
There's a very pally ballet
through the alleyways of Calais,
while the cry 'Hep-hep!'
rings round Dieppe
to a reptilian quick-step.
And . . .
dragons do any dance you can do:
fast fandango, slow soft shoe.
Two-by-two in their tutus too
they can cancan. Can you?

The drink gets stronger.
They do the conga,
embarrassingly harass
half the populace of Paris
who are rendered melancholic
by their alcoholic frolic
when they waltz their way
down the Champs Elysees.
Further from sober than from Dover,
they stagger all over,
sing 'The Wild Rover',
strut the bossa nova
cos . . .
dragons do any dance you can do:
fast fandango, slow soft shoe.
Two-by-two in their tutus too
they can cancan. Can you?

When they gavotte, it gets them hot,
makes them drink a heck of a lot,
tot on tot of heaven-knows-what
and a number of rums and in the rumba.
In the quick fox-trot, they're sick on the spot.
But . . .
dragons do any dance you can do:
fast fandango, slow soft shoe.
Two-by-two in their tutus too
they can cancan. Can you?

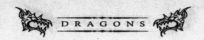

Still too ill
for a full quadrille,
they survive a lively jive.
On the boat, it's back to the bars,
smoking stacks of long cigars,
entire packs of strong Gauloise,
Sipping cognacs, advocaats,
dragons do any dance you can do:
very last tango (terribly blue),
fast fandango, slow soft shoe.
Twirl you round and swing you through.
Do-se-do and shoo-be-doo.
Two-by-two in their tutus too
they can cancan. Can you?

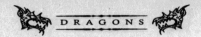
What Can a Dragon Do for a Living?

What can a dragon do for a living?
What can a dragon do?
Not get a job in London Zoo.
Not sell a skirt or a shirt or a shoe.
Not be a porter in Waterloo.
So what can a dragon . . .
What can a dragon . . .
What can a dragon do?

The problem's got him in a proper stew.
He's more hopping mad than a kangaroo.
What can a dragon . . .
What can a dragon . . . .
What can a dragon do?

He could be a cigarette lighter
But he's too big to fit in a pocket.
He could be a plane – say, a fighter –
But he's not got a gun or a rocket.
So what can a dragon . . .
What can a dragon . . .
What can a dragon do?

His breath is a fiery brew.
He could warm your house for you
But the curtains'd certainly scorch
And the furniture blacken like coke.
He might work as a light or torch
Though we'd choke in a cloak of his smoke.
So what can a dragon . . .
What can a dragon . . .
What can a dragon do
To stay off the dole queue?

He could join a security crew.
He could guard the valued possessions
Of those in positions of wealth . . .
But dragons have treasure obsessions
He'd just want it all for himself.
He'd say: 'This stuff is divine. It's ever so fine.
I'm making it mine. You can't have it back!'
So the boss would have to give him the sack.
He'd shout: 'Get out! Get out! Get out!
The dragon's no good! Now, see that he leaves.
How can we have guards who turn into thieves?'
So what can a dragon . . .
What can a dragon . . .
What can a dragon do?

When summer's well and truly through,
When rain clouds form and a storm is due,
He could be a green umbrella
But he's ever so heavy to hold.
Or maybe a newspaper seller,
But in the freezing cold,
He'd turn from green to blue.
He'd probably catch the flu,
And go: 'Achoo! Achoo! Achoo!
This job's no good, I need something new.'
So what can a dragon . . .
What can a dragon . . .
What can a dragon do?
What career can he pursue?

Well, I really wish I knew
But I simply haven't a clue.
What work have we got for the creature?
The problem is proving too tough.
He could just have a job as a teacher
But I know he's not nasty enough!
So what can a dragon . . .
What can a dragon . . .
What can a dragon do?
I dunno. Do you?

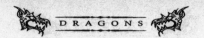

Acting as if We're Dragons

Let's imagine that we're dragons. See who's best.
Pretend you're fast asleep inside your nest . . .
Then stretch as you emerge from reptile rest . . .
Yawn . . . and growl from deep inside your
    chest . . .
Press your stomach . . . Dream of something to
    digest . . .

Shake yourself . . . and breathe out thick, black
    smoke . . .
Cough a bit . . . because it makes you choke.
Then rub your eyes . . . and move like you just
    woke . . .

Slowly stare out from your mountain lair . . .
Snarl . . . and try to make your nostrils flare . . .
Now suck . . . to fill your fiery lungs with air . . .

Let's see you exercise your lethal claws . . .
Expose those rows of teeth between your jaws . . .
Then scratch your ancient scars from dragon
    wars . . .

Stand up slowly . . . huge and hard-as-nails.
Flex those muscles underneath your scales . . .
Now set your sights on distant hills and vales . . .

And flap your arms as if they're heavy wings . . .
Listen to the way the high wind sings . . .
as you fly towards the lands of kings.

Lick your lips . . . and keep your cruel eyes
    peeled . . .
Though you need to feed, your wounds have
    hardly healed
from your fight with a knight with sword and
    shield.

You're dizzy and weak before you arrive.
This time, you wonder if you will survive.
It's dangerous to hunt in the human hive.
But hunger hurts, it stabs your guts like five
    hundred knives.
See that food below you . . .? Go into a dive . . .
Rip apart everything down there alive . . .

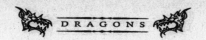

The Misunderstood Dragon

If we meet with a dragon while out walking in this
   wood,
I can't help wondering whether we should
automatically assume that he's up to no good.

Admittedly, he'd drag us off and doubtless would
make a meal of us both as quickly as he could,
crunching on our bones and licking up the blood
for supper, with gravy and mounds of mashed spud
and cabbage and carrots and Yorkshire pud.

And we'd land in a lump in his stomach with a
   thud
and slip with a squelch into pools of tummy crud,
like splashing in your wellies in a puddle of mud.
But he'd belch and say: 'Sorry!', as we sank in that
   flood.
He's not cruel – just hungry, and a bit misunder-
   stood.

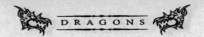
The Last Great Dragoness

The last dragon king left a daughter
who winged her way here over water.

So, for sport, so we thought, we bought guns and
    we sought her.
We hunted and hounded and cornered and caught
    her.

A lumbering, cumbersome, fiery old snorter,
she turned out far tougher than we had first
    thought her.

We gave her no quarter, but faced her and fought
    her,
lost count of the means we were forced to resort to
yet, to cut a quite cruel account shorter,
we blew her to bits with a bomb from a mortar.

But, of course, they brought in a sort of reporter,
a devious story distorter,
who wrote of a glorious slaughter.

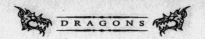
Dungeons and Dragons

– 1 –

When thrown in some deeply dark dungeon
beware of just where you are plunging.
If you smell hungry smoke
it'll be from the throat
down which you're invited, for luncheon.

– 2 –

If ever you're at such a function
do try to ignore all that munching.
They make their food suffer
so don't make it tougher
by screaming cos you're who they're crunching.

Truth and Lies About Dragons

When I look at you,
can you tell by my eyes
whether this is true
or a pack of lies?

Your Chinese dragon, chum, I'll cheerfully confirm
is a big, bright and blustery, breezy worm.
We had one at school, but it left last term,
got a good job with a Birmingham firm.

We've bird-like dragons with feathers and beaks
that nest on Peruvian mountain peaks.
They don't hoard treasure, they collect antiques
acquired from Arabs and shipped by Greeks.

There are sea-serpents in the boiling swell,
great coiling snakes from the heart of Hell,
that can tell, by smell, where to start an oil well.
They're employed by BP, Gulf and Shell.

Our English dragons, inhabit the Shires,
where everyone admires these graceful flyers.
They start the stubble fires that the squire requires,
and are famed for their fairness as cricket umpires.

Then you've got your Welsh beast, muscly and red,
with skin-n-bone wings and a brutal head.
Ivor Evans had one in his garden shed,
though he now grows daffodils and leeks instead.

When I look at you,
can you tell by my eyes
whether that was true
or a pack of lies?

Why Welsh Dragons Stopped Being Green

I know why all dragons in Wales
are red from their heads to their tails.
They once lived in trees.
Up there, by degrees,
they ripened, then fell, with red scales.

Vacancies for Dragons

'TRUE DRAGONS WANTED . . . Usual skills.
Must be good at quick clean kills.'
I need a job to pay my bills.
I don't wanna work in shops or mills.
I want danger. I want thrills.
I wanna indulge my hunger pangs.
I wanna scare people with my fangs.
I wanna hang around with scaly gangs.

'DRAGONS WANTED . . . Dangerous tasks.
Wouldn't suit humans wearing masks.'
That's how the advert read.
Now, I've not got the body, not got the head.
But . . .
I could be a dragon.
I'm dead keen.
I could be
miserly
cruel and mean,
cursed, blood-thirsty,
the worst there's been.

'REAL DRAGONS WANTED . . . Demanding
   work.
Requires much more than a smoke-stained smirk.'
So they said
but they're misled
cos . . .
I could be a dragon.
That's my scene.
I could eat
people-meat
for the protein.
And if I grew a new skin
it'd be green.

'DRAGONS WANTED . . . Difficult posts.
No time-wasters with idle boasts.
No badly bred.
No ghostly dead.'
So why don't they choose me instead?
Cos
I could be a dragon.
I'd be wild,
crave a cave
where bones are piled,
have the whole place
horribly styled.
Rip you open
if you smiled.
So don't you dare,
you dreadful child!
I can be awful
when I'm riled.

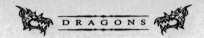

The Disappearance of Chinese Dragons

Three thousand miles from the Philippine Isles
to the heights of Turkestan,
and all the way from Mandalay
to the coast of far Japan

you'll find depicted and displayed
dragons of every shape and shade
embroidered, painted, carved in jade,
in ivory, pearl or wood-inlaid.
Their past was treasure. Their future's trade.
They're only worth the price that's paid.

From copper mines and camel lines
on dry Mongolia's barren plains
to Buddhist prayer and Yeti lair
on high Tibetan mountain chains

the dragon that they now parade's
a paper one which people made.
The actual creature's long decayed,
its spirit cheapened and betrayed
with paste and paint that time will fade;
its world of wonderment, mislaid.

No egg, no bone, no trace remains.
An empty throne where silence reigns.
A twilight zone. All loss, no gains.
The bird has flown. The old moon wanes.
No crop is grown: no fruit, no grains.
Its ghost is blown through these terrains.

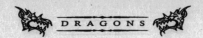

The Capturing of a Dragon

He reared up before me,
his body bright green;
a serpent with legs,
if you know what I mean.

The moment I caught him,
I thought him quite ruthless;
though dragons have teeth,
and this one was toothless.

His scales were so fine that
they looked just like hair.
His wings were so tiny
they weren't really there.

He wasn't quite able
to demonstrate flight.
His breath wasn't fiery.
It didn't ignite.

And he didn't breathe smoke,
or let out a roar.
And he hadn't a tail,
nor hint of a claw.

He didn't hoard treasure
or cause maidens grief.
He didn't eat people,
just chewed on a leaf;

was not very lengthy,
and not at all tall;
in fact, was not biggish,
but actually quite small.

He lived in a matchbox.
I called him Godzilla . . .
. . . not much of a dragon,
but a great caterpillar!

Dragons Don't Exist

Dragons, mate? They don't exist.
So cross them off your Xmas list.

We've no such things –
no snakes with wings.

Ask any archaeologist
if dragons do or don't exist.
He'll treat you like you're round the twist.
So pardon me if I insist
that dragons simply don't exist.

We've no such things –
no snakes with wings,
no spikes, no scales,
no pointed tails.

If any college scientist
suggested that they *might* exist
then he or she would be dismissed.
Not me, cos I'm a realist.
I *know* that dragons don't exist.

We've no such things –
no snakes with wings,
no spikes, no scales,
no pointed tails,
no sudden death
by fiery breath,

no flying oral arsonist.
'The creature simply can't exist,'
says teacher and says naturalist.
It's pure Scotch mist so let's desist
cos dragons simply don't exist.

We've no such things –
no snakes with wings,
no spikes, no scales,
no pointed tails,
no sudden death
by fiery breath,
no rich rewards,
no treasure hoards.

The Blarney Stone must have been kissed
by those insisting they exist.
Oi! See this fist above my wrist?
It's yours right now if you persist,
cos dragons truly don't exist.

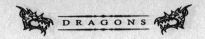

He led us to
the dragon's lair,
said: 'I'll show you!'
and walked in there.

Then came a roar,
a scream, a moan,
and nothing more
was ever known

or missed
of the man who said dragons
didn't exist.

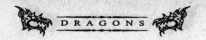

Evidence

Dragon in computer games.
Places bearing dragon names.
Dragon used as skin tattoo.
Ship to carry Viking crew.
Sleeping now, but when it wakes,
starts up storms and makes earthquakes.

Dragon drawn on early maps.
Gardens where the dragon snaps.
Ponds patrolled by dragonflies.
Dragon donning human guise.
Serpent circling the globe.
Dragon on a Chinese robe.

Dragon flown as paper kite.
Effigy in tribal rite.
Dragon as a kids' cartoon.
Origin of word 'dragoon'.
Dragon that the hero slew.
Biggest thing that ever flew.

Dragon landing on your roof.
You still saying: 'Bring me proof!'

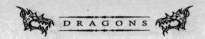

Rare Dragons

You'll seldom find a dragon with
no trace of the barbarian,
a sentimental gentle one
who's not a slightly scary one.

There's surely not a dragon that
is purely vegetarian,
that really cares for animals
and is a veterinarian.

Or one that looks at lots of books,
a qualified grammarian,
that has a love of literature
and works as a librarian.

No shaven-headed Buddhist nor
your peaceful, hippy, hairy one,
nor one that's into reggae who's
a dreadlocked Rastafarian.

The Birth of a Dragon

Into the belly of the nest
she'd built in the bleak north-west
the mother-dragon pressed
an egg as big as a whisky-keg.

And leaves grew dark on oak and yew,
while her offspring fed on yolk, and grew.
Then a crack in the shell and, poking through,
came a claw, a few more, then a leg.

And the whole egg broke in two
and from the shell came half the smell of Hell

and with it a beast without place or time,
like a word which will not write or rhyme.
So there it lay, encased in slime,
for a while, then raised a head that was vile.

No natural nightmare could compile
this child, with eyes as wide and wild
as the seas which swirl round all these isles,
and a cry which reaches miles and miles.

And lightning, flashing over beaches,
comes from flaming, flickering tongues;
while thunder, galloping from lungs,
terrorises creatures.

Life and Death

They felt few emotions.
Their blood was corrosive.
Their dreams were deep oceans.
Their breath was explosive.

Their land lay uncharted.
Their caves were like sewers.
Their sleep was hardhearted.
Their claws were like skewers.

Their hunger was boundless.
Their lives, melodrama.
Their flight was quite soundless.
Their scales were their armour.

Their tails were like rivers.
Their flames like bright fountains.
Their cries caused cold shivers.
Their wealth was worth mountains.

Their instinct was grasping.
Their airspace was birdless.
Their voices were rasping.
Their language was wordless.

Their eyes were like lasers.
Their minds were infernal.
Their teeth were like razors.
Their wisdom eternal.

Their fighting ferocious.
Their battleground blazing.
Their deaths were atrocious.
Though they were amazing.

How We Dealt With Dangerous Dragons

According
to history's recorders,
most dragons were hoarders
with wingspreads as broad as
from here to the borders.
These dangerous marauders
had mental disorders.

Their victims implored us
and swore to reward us.
They said: 'Please afford us
help. All have ignored us,
not even insured us.'

We heard them applaud us
when mad dragons roared as
we caged them, with warders,
the same way the law does:
Big warders with orders
to keep them secured as
safe as a gun or a sword is.

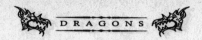

Finding a Dragon's Lair

The way to find a dragon's lair
is down the road that goes nowhere,
over the bridge of Curse-And-Swear
on the river of Deep Despair.

Take the track to Give-You-A-Scare
across the marsh of Say-A-Prayer,
over the peak of Past Repair
and down the cliff of Do Beware.

Through the valley of If-You-Dare
you'll find the town of Don't-Go-There
where folk won't speak but stand and stare
and nobody will be Lord Mayor.

Beyond lies land that's parched and bare,
a dried-up lake named None-To-Spare,
a rock that's known as Life's Unfair
and hills they call No-Longer-Care.

It's hard to breathe the dreadful air
and in the sun's relentless glare
the heat becomes too much to bear.
You'll not be going anywhere.

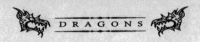

You're weak and dazed but just aware
of something moving over there
approaching to inspect its snare.
And then you smell the dragon's lair.